Dot

Patricia Intriago

Margaret Ferguson Books | Farrar Straus Giroux | New York

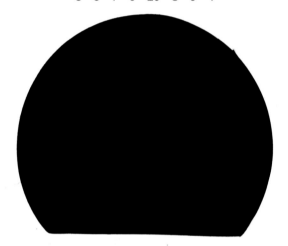

Library of Congress Cataloging-in-Publication Data

Intriago, Patricia.
    Dot / Patricia Intriago. — 1st ed.
        p.   cm.
    Summary: Pairs of circular shapes convey opposite relationships in the arc of a day.
    ISBN: 978-0-374-31835-2
    [1. Stories in rhyme.   2. Circle—Fiction.   3. English language—Synonyms and antonyms—
Fiction.]   I. Title.

PZ8.3.I6274Do 2011
[E]—dc22
                                                                            2010019816

Dot

Stop dot

Go dot

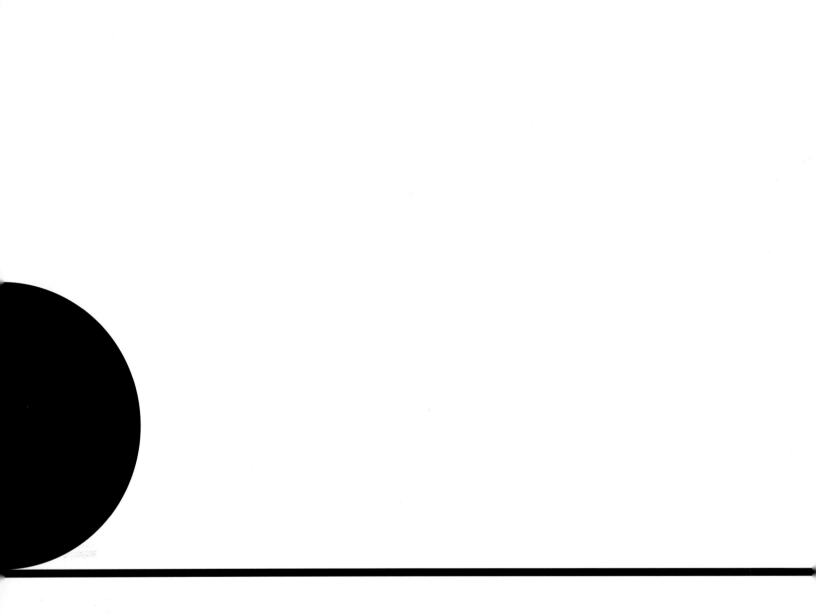

Slow dot

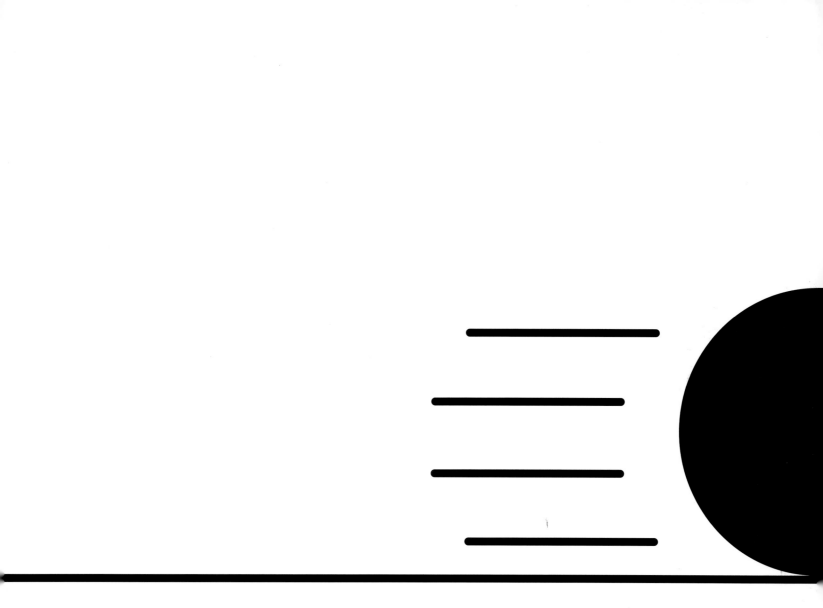

Fast dot

Up and down dots
bounce around

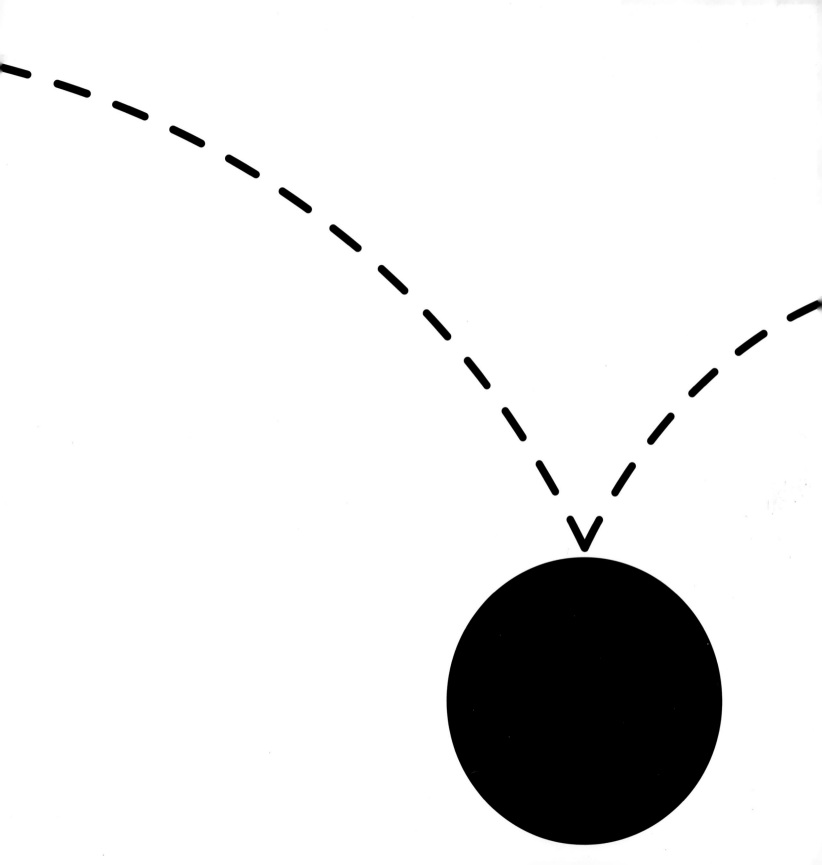

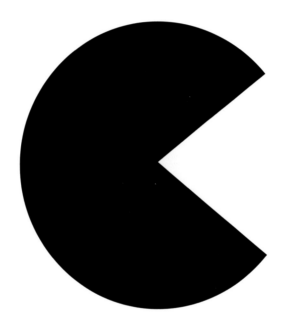

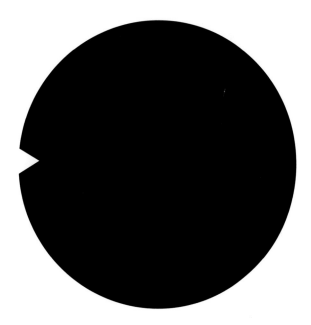

Loud and quiet dots
make different sounds

Heavy dot

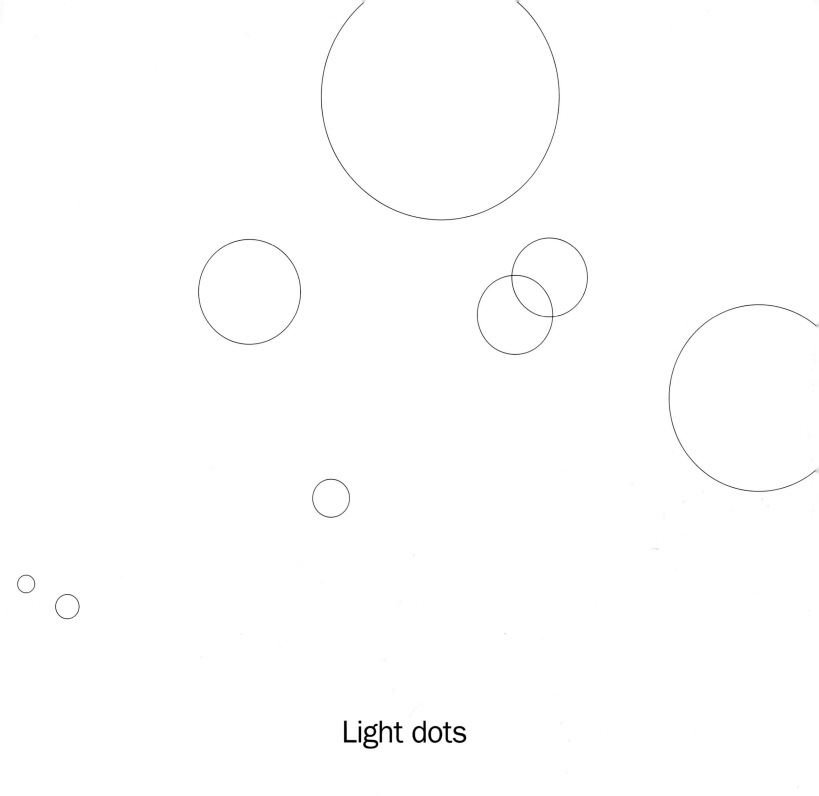

Light dots

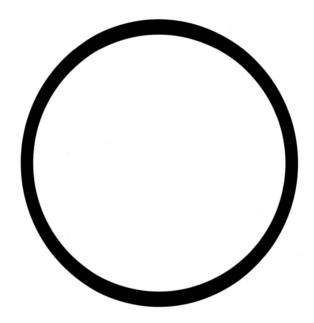

Hungry dot

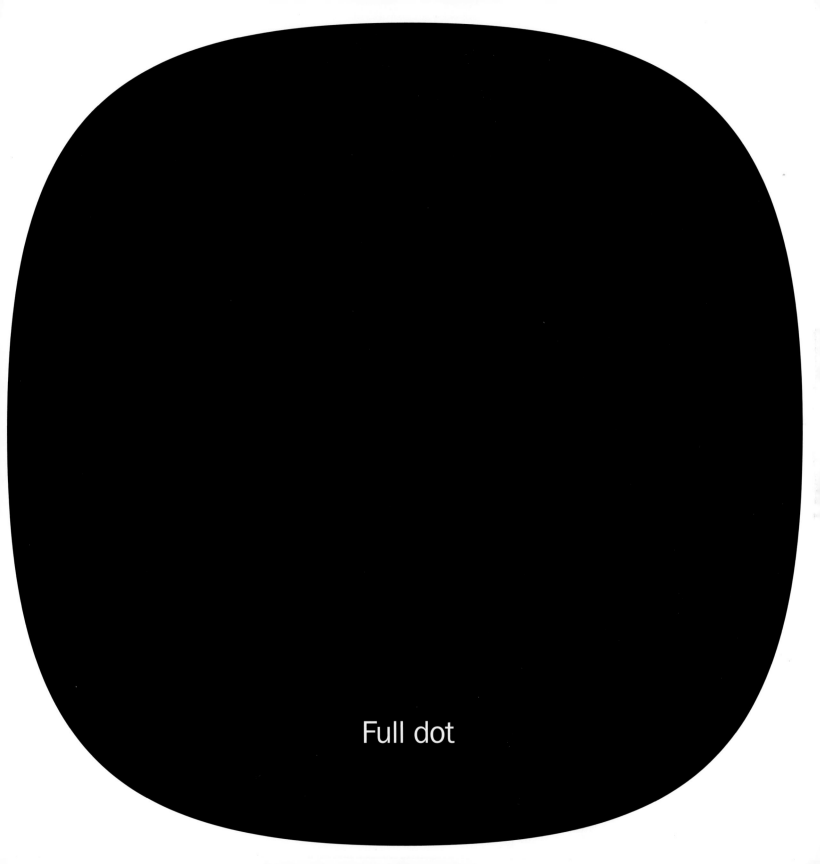

Full dot

This dot is happy

This dot is sad

This dot is yummy

This dot tastes bad

Hard dot

Soft dot

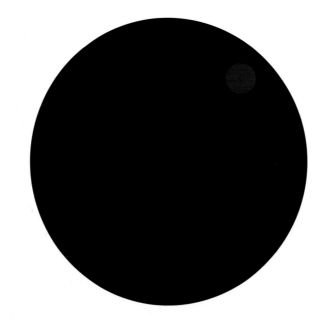

Hurt dot

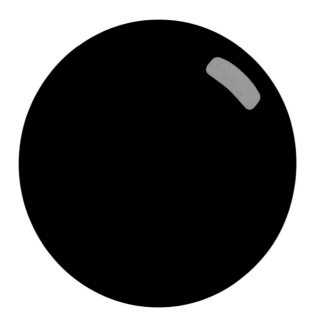

Heal dot

Got dots

Not dots

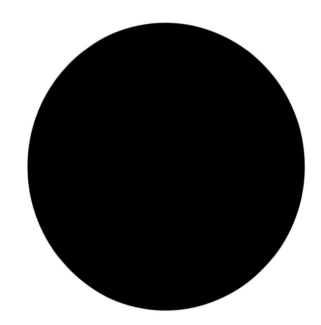

Do you see a shy dot?

Dot here

Dot there

Lots of dots everywhere

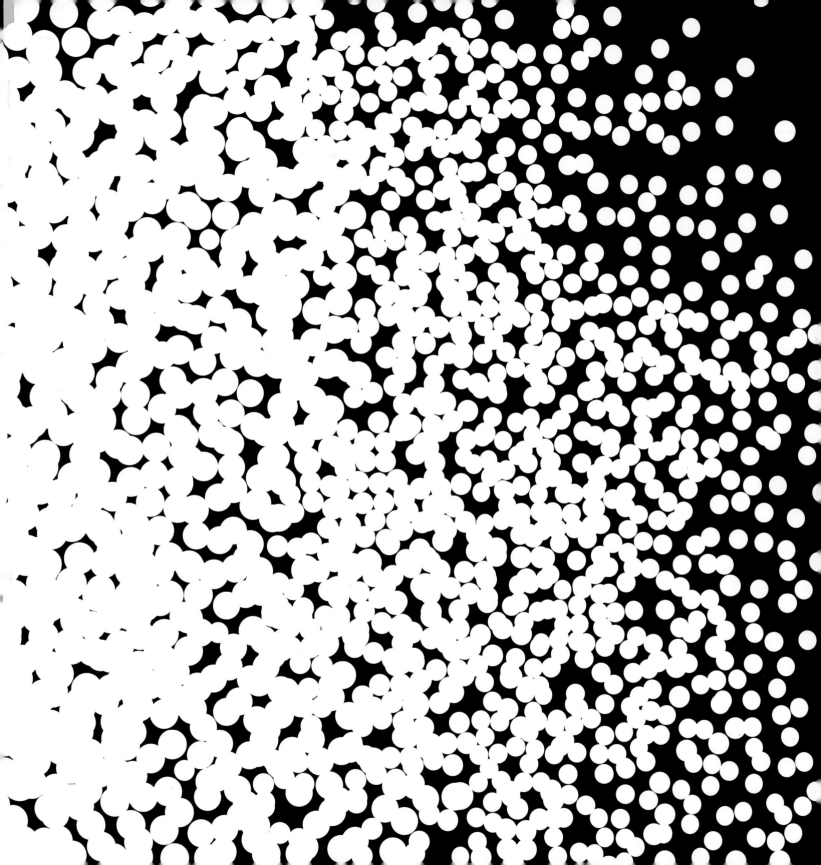

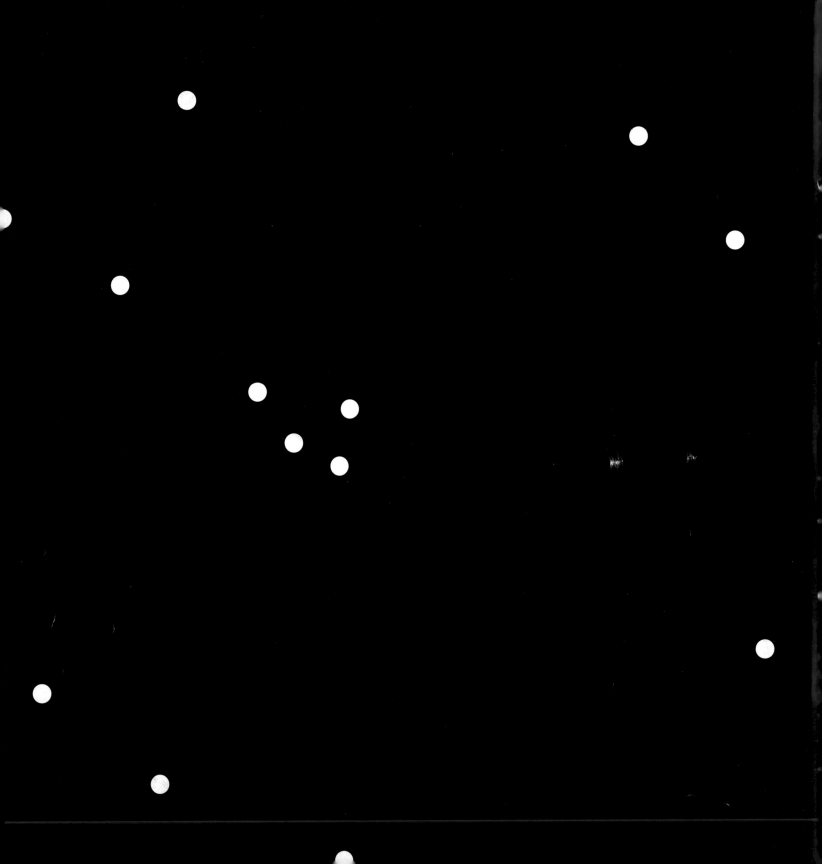

Dots up in the sky so bright
twinkle as we say good night